PARANORMAL SEX COLLECTION VOLUME 1

EXPLICIT DIRTY EROTICA SHORT STORIES

BLAINE TELLER

plicit Press

CHAPTER 1

A HEATED HAUNTING

THERE WASN'T any denying the shadow in the mirror. It was a man, a large man. The coat on him gave away that he was from another time, another century. I couldn't make out his face clearly but he had deep-set eyes and a beard. The room was suddenly ice cold and even the mirror misted, and then frosted. Still, I wasn't scared, moving in towards the looking glass so that I could get a better look. I didn't want to look back, the confirmation that this would bring too much for me at the moment. I couldn't believe that they were right about the house being haunted.

Leaning over, I circled the misty mirror; making round windows through which I could peep at what I was now sure was a ghost behind me. I had had a million questions before coming into the bathroom, the most haunted room in this old Manhattan walk-up, but now all I could think of was that they had all been right on the money. I keep reminding myself that my name is Lauren as if this will confirm for me my own sanity. I keep staring through the parts of the mirror. I keep clearing with my sleeve but surprise myself at my lack of fear. Instead, I'm a mixture of excited and unexpectedly aroused. My vagina sends warm whispers up through my belly and my hand moves from the glass to my cunt, the ghost behind me moving closer.

Before I can decide to leave the room and take care of my beating clit in the safety of my un-haunted hotel room a few blocks down the road, a dark, dense mass fills the space. One more look into the mirror and I see nothing. The man is gone. There isn't time to question the reality of what I think I saw because what I do see is suddenly all around me. As the black envelopes me I'm surprised that it is less like a cloudy smoke and more like an actual force. I feel it on my skin as I've felt so many touches so many times before. For the first time, I'm scared.

I try to scream, but it's impossible. Nothing but the strain of screaming is felt, no sound. I hear the others in the tour moving around just outside. I hear someone struggle with the door handle. I hear another person, a guide I think, confirming that the door gives trouble occasionally. They call for me and then confirm to each other that I must have moved to another part of the house. I try in vain to let them know that I'm in the bathroom with what is now a black cloud that has the ability to touch me. I see the panic register on my face just as my chest slams down onto the counter, my head to the side and my arms spread out on either side of me, my hands also flat on the counter.

There is a rush up my legs, like cold water being hosed onto them from behind and beneath. My legs slide apart, to about a foot, and then my G-string starts rolling down of its own accord, the cold rush instantly on my pussy and inside my ass. The pressure increases steadily from that of a garden hose to what I would imagine a fireman's hose to feel like. Thankfully, the cold rush becomes warmer as the seconds tick by. Or I could just be adjusting to the cold. I shiver as the temperature on me changes, but soon enough the warmth is all over me like my favorite coat.

I can't look down at my pussy but suddenly it feels like a thousand tongues are on it. Solid licks cover my pussy and immediately my cunt is on fire. I want to know who it is that is eating out my pussy in the dark. It can't be the shadowy apparition with the beard. It just can't be. But whoever, whatever it is doing one stellar fucking job on my vagina and I'm dripping through my panic. I don't care who it is, I just know that I don't want them to stop.

Suddenly I'm off the counter, standing straight up, facing the mirror. I watch as the buttons on my blouse undo themselves, and then my strapless bra. I watch the lace fall from my breasts and then gasp as fingers are on my tits. The invisible fingers make known their path, leaving deep red impressions in their wake. I watch my boobs parted and lifted. I watch as my nipples are squeezed between my fingertips. I strain for some glimpse of the hands doing such a good job of sealing my desire to be fucked by this invisible force but see only the effect on my breasts of the activity sending shards of fuck-me-now through my entire body.

I want to look down. I want to see who is busy on my cunt. But I must assume that the same invisible fingers on my breasts are the very same working my pussy now as it feels like the lips that cover the opening to my vagina are pulled apart and my cunt is entered by what feels like four fingers. There is a weight on my shoulders that presses me down onto the fingers that push up forcefully into my cunt. I still can't scream. I don't want to. But at least I'm allowed to breathe. The fingers move deeper and deeper into me.

Then they move around wildly inside of me, the press on my shoulders still firm. I catch my face in the mirror and if whatever it is that is finger fucking me catches the same reflection, it knows that I'm enjoying every second of this poltergeist assault.

I'm fucked firm for a good while and then suddenly I'm off the ground. Again, I panic as I watch myself lift up into the air. My legs rise up to the position they would be in if I was sitting on a low stool. My arms are again stretched out to either side of me. I see now that my underwear is around my ankles. My skirt rolls now to form a perfect band around my waist. I watch as my breasts again become the focus, my legs parting slowly until I can almost see right into my cunt. I'm so fucking aroused now, probably a fear response, that my cunt drips pussy-lava onto the floor. I start to plead in my head because it won't come out of my mouth for this thing, whatever it is, to fuck me. In my head, I imagine it to be the bearded ghost I saw. I need it to be something and so I make it him.

The pressure around my cunt and on my cunt is suddenly intense. I can't look at my pussy by turning my head in the appropriate direction but my eyes find my hole reflecting back to me in the mirror. There's a complete vulnerability that I feel now that the feeling of support under my ass disappears. Still, I do not fall. The feeling is that I am hanging by strong support under my arms. I am being held up more than I am hanging down. There is secondary support under my knees as though I am sitting on the lap of a very large man. I am the shape appearing in brief hazes now as I stare at my pussy, which is being threatened now by the most incredible pressure. The feeling is of an incredibly thick cock trying to get inside me. I want it.

The apparition responds to my desires and I can no

longer think of myself as being fucked by a ghost. It feels every bit like a man. It is a man. I feel the grain of his beard against the side of my face, tenderly brushing against my cheek. I inhale deeply as my vaginal lips part and the tiny hole begin to stretch open in an almost perfect circle. Suddenly my arms are mine again and instinctively I wrap them around the invisible torso before me. This brings what can only be lips on my neck, cheeks, and then my lips. I kiss back, my eyes fixed on my steadily expanding punani.

The cock is inside me now, moving forward and upwards. I can see into my cunt almost completely. There is something disturbing about this visual but this eerie sense lasts only until the dick starts thrusting. My tight squeeze is reciprocated and the almost crushing strength of the arms around me is enough to keep me up now as the support under my legs too is lost. The only support I have below my waist now is the pounding penis in my pussy. Repeatedly I fall onto the dick pushing up into me, my shoulders held tightly so that I'm constantly in range of the dick giving me the most pleasure I've ever had in my life. I want to scream but know now that this is not allowed. I take this delicious punishment in silent moans, my cunt exploding.

I can't watch now as my cunt feels like it is being pulled from inside. I don't want to see what I don't need to see. The feeling is sufficient for me, so I close my eyes. Places inside my vagina that I had never had tapped before are being absolutely pounded now, my head not able to process these million first-time experiences. I have never been fucked so deep, and still, all I want is more. If it was possible for me to do anything with my body of my own accord, I would push down on this massive invisible rod inside me. Part of me wishes even that I could be on my back so that I could be totally dominated by this massive bearded poltergeist.

There is an expansion in my pussy now that would suggest that the cock inside it has doubled in thickness. I gag, almost breathless, as it seems to double in length as well. It seems that every desire inside me is responded to by the appropriate part of the body of my pussy-plugging menace. There is nothing more that I want now as my cunt is overstretched and milked by more cock than I would ever have imagined possible. I dare not imagine more, giving myself instead to where we are now. Content with the proceedings in my cunt I wonder how long it will be before the ghost inside me climaxes, and if my own orgasm will be led to progressively or if it will be yanked from me with the rest of my cunt.

Every muscle in my cunt pulls tightly as I start to cum. I don't expect it, usually able to read my own body. But suddenly I am cumming with more force than even the cock inside me is fucking me with. Every square inch of the surface of my skin explodes in beautiful unison as my entire body culminates in one massive orgasm. For a minute I have no idea where I am, and even that my name is Lauren. I know just that the pounding in my pussy and the beating of my heart are one, the rhythm consistent and intense. For the instant that I open my eyes, I see that the size of the hole that is my cunt gets smaller. This is not because the cock inside it is shrinking, or because it is exiting. It is because the force of my climax strengthens my vagina such that it squeezes so tightly on the cock that it almost completely closes around it.

As my climax draws to a close I am flat on my back in mid-air, and then my back arched. There is a rapid thrusting now so that I know that even my fuck-buddy is about to blow. A final deep thrust and the cock settle for a long while in the back of my pussy and pulsates for a bit. The slow withdrawal of the cock is a delicious punishment. I love it. I'm lowered to the floor now, my back and ass on the cold tiles. The density in the room lifts, the light returning. I fumble with my panties just as someone on the other side of the door fumbles with the handle.

CHAPTER 2

A VAMPIRES FIRST LOVER (PARANORMAL EROTIC)

FEW PEOPLE ever really understand what it is like to be a vampire. Those that see us and hear about us all have one thing in their mind. They think we are this race of ruthless killers who hunt for food and kill with little to no regard for human life. The truth of the matter is that we are not as the movies and television shows have portrayed us to be. We are actually a race of species that are no different from you. One example of this was my first lover that I took. Let me start from the beginning. My name is Vlad Popavich and I am a vampire. I am around 300 years old but look no more than twenty-five. I would like to share my story about how I came to take my first lover and show that what you have heard about us is a great stretch than the truth. My tale is more of a love story than anything else. The sex, I must admit, was incredible, but deep down there was true love in the person, and I swear that they would have been mine forever.

. . .

The story about how I was made is not as important as the story of the love between Steafania and me.

I was in a bar one night just sitting and having a few drinks. That is the one thing that being a vampire has given me, is the ability to drink and not be affected. This has to be done in moderation. If I drink too much and tend to not show signs of being affected, then it will cause questions to be asked and I have a lot of explaining to do. Anyway, I was sitting there taking in the many conversations that were going on, and then I saw Steafania walk in. I had to admit that at first, she was not that much to look at, but she had a quality that I was not able to get past. I sensed something from her the moment that she first walked into the door. I sat there a little longer and studied everything about her, the way that she walked and the way that she handled herself caused me to be almost in a trance around her. She walked to the other end of the bar and had a seat. After she had been there a while, I walked over and began to talk to her. I wanted to know this woman's life story; I was taken by her and was all about wanting to know what I could learn about her.

Steafania sat there and began to talk to me a little more with each passing minute. After a couple of hours, I almost felt that she and I had a connection and that we were meant to be together. Steafania suggested that we head back to her place where we were able to talk more and get to know one another more intimately. I went back to Steafania's place. I had to admit that she was quite the collector of old antiques. I sat down while she poured us a couple of drinks for us to share while we talked and enjoyed the company of one another. She told me about the harsh upbringing that I could almost relate to, as mine had also been difficult. I was surprised at the way that Steafania and I were able to relate on such a close level. I was amazed at the number of things in our life that seemed to line up almost perfectly. The talking led to us being closer and things getting to be a lot more personal and intimate between the two of us. Steafania made the first move by taking her hand and placing it on my leg. The feeling of her touching me made me feel even more that what was going on between me and her was magic. I was almost not able to refrain myself any longer and almost took her at the moment. I returned the favor by gently caressing her face and neck.

Steafania took my hand and led it down to her ample breasts that were all but begging for some serious attention from me. Part of me was nervous while the other part of me wanted to just dive in and ravish her. I took my hand and found my way into her top. I was getting quite aroused at the thought of taking my fangs and sinking my teeth into her ample flesh. I felt the end of her nipple quickly become hard and erect at my touch. I gave it a little twist and watched as Steafania reacted as a sign of approval. Steafania quickly suggested that we lose our clothes and just let our animalistic nature come out. The woman I met only a few hours earlier was suggesting we start fucking our brains out until we were both unable to lift a finger. I was fine with this suggestion and did not see anything wrong with this idea.

. . .

Steafania led me to her room where she laid on her back with her legs spread in an open invitation to have my way with her freshly shaved love tunnel. I dove down into position. I began to lick and insert my tongue into her wet slit. The taste of her juices on my tongue was almost too much for me to even bare. I got more and more excited with each passing moment that I could tell that her wetness was getting more and more intense. Steafania was more and more on the verge of having a sexual experience that she never thought possible. I was ready to give her the thrill of a lifetime and decided to head up and go back to working over her nipples while I took the time to begin pounding her tight hole. I was unable to believe that she was as tight as she was. It was almost as if I was pounding a virgin for the very first time. I was able to feel her pussy gripping onto my cock and my foreskin sliding up and down the length of my 9" cock. The sensation was unlike anything that I had ever felt and I almost felt bad that I was going to have to bite her and turn her into one of my children. It was something that had to be done and regardless of what I thought, it had to be done for her sake as well as for my continued existence as I had not fed and was getting weak.

Steafania let out a moan that was not like anything I had ever heard. She was begging me to fuck her harder and not stop until I had filled her with a load of my thick and creamy cum. I continued this for another few minutes until I released deep inside of her. After this, I made my move and went in and bit her neck. I had made Steafania into one of my children.

. . .

A few months later, I had a terrible feeling that something bad had happened to Steafania. I tried to pass it off but something kept eating at me that there was something that had happened to her and that the connection between me and her had been lost. I found out that my feelings had been right as she had fallen victim to a vampire hunter that took the time to torture her before he killed her. Even though she is gone, I will never forget my one true vampire love.

CHAPTER 3

AND THE LION ROARED

ALLUCIAN WATCHED the sun sink like a glowing ball of orange fire between the distant mountain peaks. He felt the familiar stirring deep inside him that he felt for the first time that one day a year ago when the pounding in his chest was demanding to be let out. He had always known this secret. On that moonlit night now so long ago he had first felt the change within begin. It began as a flutter in the pit of his blond-haired stomach and rippled up through his chest to grip his mind with a fever that tore through him like some guttural ancient scream. He had watched the change many times until his eyes grew red from the boiling blood coursing through his veins. It was a time of need, the kind of need that tears away the fabric of sanity and leaves behind the beast.

Aretheal felt the sun sink as well from the other side of the Great River that wound between the mountains. She had been waiting for this night and looked with hopeful eyes towards where she knew Allucian could feel the beast within purr. Her dark reddish-blond hair lay full across her back against her supple skin. She saw the last rim of the sun disappear beneath the horizon and felt her stomach shudder, her green eyes in the mirror beginning to redden around the edges as the need began to overtake her as well.

The night found them both racing towards the grassy plain they met at every year on this night of nights. His dark mane flowed like quicksilver as his powerful tawny legs pulled the grasslands beneath him. He was a streak of streamlined shadow in the fading darkness as the moon inched higher above the hills behind him. Aretheal too slipped through the swaying grass with a muffled hiss as she plunged towards the small clearing beside the pool in the middle of their secret place. Her heart pounded as her long legs ate yards of ground with each urgent stride, filling her body with an energy that only the two of them could comprehend. She could see the lone Baobab tree in the distance that signaled the end of the journey was near. Her pace became a tawny blur as her blood-red eyes strained to see her mate.

Allucian broke through the head-high curtain of grass into the clearing to see Aretheal burst into sight from the far side of the field heading straight for the single giant of ancient times towering beside the clear spring that reflected the moon's beams like arrows from the mirror-smooth surface of the spring. They both sprang as one their bodies stretched out in mid-air, their crimson eyes locked on each other with hunger neither animal-human nor beast could ever know. Their journey was complete as they landed beside each other with a muffled thump.

Allucian stood in the full moonlight as he had so many times and felt the transformation once again grip him, his taut flesh rippling as he stood there a full six feet tall, his naked body almost shuddering with need. His cock had grown stiff and curved like some flesh scimitar, his arousal clear liquid evidence upon its tip, his balls lying heavy beneath the base of the shaft. He leaned his head back and snarled out in defiance to the moon, his arms thrust skyward into the still-hot African night.

Aretheal rose up upon her hind feet and flexed her shoulders back, her long reddish hair glistening in the gleaming moonlight. Her breasts stood firm and full, their tips now achingly hard as they puffed out like swollen rose-buds tingling almost beyond imagination. Her pussy was swollen tenderness, fully furred with thick darkened curls, her long inner lips like draped surrender and they jutted out from the dense mass of hair. She could smell the demand that oozed from between her legs as she slowly strode to her lover's side.

They met at the edge of the water, Allucian's long tongue encircling her erect nipples until she purred with excitement. Arethal's fingers curled around his cock and squeezed it as she buried her head into his fluffy furry chest. She pulled it between her fingers until its tip with cupped in her palm. Slowly she sank to her knees, slipped the nut of his cock head into her hot mouth, and sucked. She looked up at him to see his eyes now boiling red as his passions began to take hold. She cupped his pendulous balls in her hands and pulled them towards her. Allucian arched his back and roared into the moonlit night as his mate suckled at his pounding shaft. He slipped to the ground beside her and with a careful but powerful thrust of his arm rolled her into the thick matt of yellow grass.

Allucian's tongue trailed up along the inside of Aretheal's thigh and stopped at the edge of her quivering cunt lips. Slowly he parted them almost with an insane need for her juice. When his broad powerful tongue swirled between her trembling lips, she arched her back and her haunting roar echoed off into the night. His tongue found her swollen bud of red agony as he greedily pulled it deep into his mouth. Her hips rose from the bed of grass driving her creamy cunt against his powerful face. It was all Allucian could take and with a sudden flip of his wide hand turned her onto her stomach.

Aretheal needed no coaxing and immediately her hands and knees were digging into the yellow grass, her hips pressed back spreading her soaked cunt lips letting her aromatic arousal waft upon the wind to Allucian's sensitive nose. Allucian's powerful hands settled onto her hips and with a flex of his powerful hips drove the full length of his cock into her willing cunt. He could feel her inner walls collapsing onto his cock as they milked his long shaft from within. Each thrust was harder, deeper until each meeting of their flesh drove her face tight against the soft grass.

Their rhythm became almost violent as Allucian pounded her sopping wet cunt beneath the moonlight. He knew the moment was near as well as Aretheal knew it from beneath him. She could feel her wet folds convulsing as her pooled juices coated his shaft with a gleaming white layer of satisfaction beneath the mystical moon above. She looked back between her legs and saw his huge balls swaying as he pounded into her from behind. Watching them slap against her began the purr from deep within her that would grow into a savage snarl and then into a roar. Allucian felt it too; it was what they had both waited for 364 days to share. He reached down beneath her hips and pulled her ass up high in line with his final thrust.

Allucian's back arched as he drove his spurting cock deep into Aretheral's creaming cunt and their bodies jerked as if jabbed with pinpricks. Allucian looked down at Aretheal's back and slowly saw the tawny fur begin to fill in her smooth skin. Her chest swelled as the muscles beneath returned to their fully furred completion. Her short reddish mane grew once again full across her shoulders. Allucian looked down to see his own stomach hair grow thick and matted as his cock pulled out of Aretheal and began to grow soft.

The mating was complete. Deep within Aretheal's cunt, Allucian's sperm were already headed for their destiny. The moon knew a special secret that night. Of the spawning of the legend that boiled in the eyes and blood of their parents. Allucian leaned down to lick the trail of his sperm than trickled out and down Aretheal's red-blond fur. With a throaty growl that turned into an anguished plea against the torture they suffered, each turned and slowly made their way across the small open field. As they always did, they paused at the edge of the grass curtain that would cover their trail like a woven weave of solid brown. They roared at each other, Aretheal's sounding a bit more somber than before, for deep inside she knew what had become her life now rested deep within her womb.

They made their way back to their beds and fell asleep as the sun poked its way up over the horizon. Allucian now lay naked fleshed and smooth as he slept upon the cool silken sheets, his heavy breaths reverberated through the already hot humidity that would drench his worn-out body with a glistening sheen.

Far from sight across the horizon, Aretheal lay naked on her bed, her rosebud nipples once again congested into puffy cones as she slept in total exhaustion. The coming year would be forever when they awoke. But that too is the fate of the lion's wrath.

Until he'd met Veronica, Jack had thought vampires were a myth. Now as he looked into her vivid amber eyes, he knew better. He swallowed and looked down at her beautiful mouth. She smiled and two sharp fangs were revealed. They might frighten some people but Jack wanted to feel their razor-sharp points pierce his skin.

Roni had promised him for weeks that she would take him to new heights of ecstasy but only when she felt he was ready. Now as she took his cock in her hand and rubbed lightly up and down, he hoped the time had come.

The sensual spell that she always weaved around him was in full force that night. She made him want her desperately and he reached down to cup a full breast and to tease the sensitive tip. Roni said, "Mmm," and covered his hand with hers.

"Squeeze it," she said.

Jack closed his hand around the perfectly formed flesh and kneaded it as though he were working over a lump of dough at the bakery where he worked. Roni practically purred as he brushed a thumb over her nipple and then rolled it between his fingers.

He and Roni were highly compatible in bed, both liking it rather rough. Pain and pleasure seemed to go hand in hand for them and they'd been happy to discover this in each other. When they fucked, they always went at each other like wild animals.

Jack grabbed her other breast and gave it the same treatment, tormenting Roni as he teased the nipples and kneaded them hard. In response, Roni started working his dick harder, almost too hard, but he loved it. Soon the head of his cock was red and swollen and Jack wanted to cum, but held it back. It was way too soon.

Roni released him as she smiled up into his blue eyes. She thought his eyes were beautiful and was glad to see them brimming with passion. Jack caught her off guard when he pushed her roughly, sending her tumbling back onto the bed. She growled at him playfully as he crawled on top of her.

Jack grabbed her hair and bent her neck back. "Spread that cunt open, bitch," he commanded.

It was another thing they enjoyed, their name-calling and rough talk. Roni liked a strong hand and Jack was happy to supply it. It was surprising in a mortal, Roni mused as she opened her legs wide and leaned back. Most mortal men she fucked were weak and tried to be romantic. She wanted no part of that. Roni wanted it hard and nasty.

Jack smacked her pussy just hard enough to sting then rubbed his fingers hard over her clit. Roni gasped and moved her hips. Jack kept it up until just before she came and then stopped. Roni's hips still moved. She needed to cum but she knew Jack was going to torture her and she welcomed it.

Taking his hard, pulsing cock in his hand, Jack slapped it against Roni's clit several times. Again Roni was on the verge of an orgasm when Jack stopped. Jack saw that Roni's eyes were beginning to glow a dull orange and he smiled at her horniness.

"Want me to fuck it, bitch?" he asked.

"Yeah, you fucker. Fuck it now," she ordered.

Jack thrust forward and the head of his cock stroked over her clit. "Like
  that?"

Roni shivered as bliss almost overtook her. She was so close, perched on the edge. It always amazed her that Jack made her so horny so fast. "Yeah. Stroke it with your prick, fucker."

Jack rocked forward again and the silky skin of his dickhead slid over the sensitive bud. Roni shivered again and Jack moved a little faster. She jerked and whimpered with a lusty hunger. She needed the release she knew Jack would give her. She watched his cock sliding over her clit and it excited her even more.

"Do it right there," she said.

Jack arched a brow at her. "Do it right there, what?"

Roni snarled at him. "Do it right there, please," she answered. "That's a good girl."

Jack decided it was time to give her what she needed and increased his tempo. Roni began to moan loudly, and then her moans grew higher in pitch until she gave a scream as her body shuddered in an intense climax. Jack didn't give her time to come down from the high. Instead, he thrust his cock deep inside of Roni, banging her hard.

He grabbed her thighs and pushed them wide. "Take it, slut," he growled at

her.

Another feminine growl rolled out of her mouth. "Give it to me, you bastard.

Give me all of that cock."

Jack squeezed her thighs hard as he pounded away at her. "Play with your clit. Let me see you stroke it."

Roni slid her hand down and rubbed her fingers over her clit hard. "Yeah, do it. Do it and cum around my cock," Jack ordered.

Roni rubbed faster and rocketed into an orgasm. Jack felt her pussy spasm around him and reveled in the way it felt.

He took his penis out and said, "On your knees and spread it."

Roni tossed him a mock scathing look and rolled over.

Barely was her ass in the air when Jack was spanking her cheeks. The sting of his palm connecting with her flesh was exquisite and Roni cried out.

"Like that, cunt?" "Yeah! Harder!"

Jack hit her ass with more force, leaving red marks on her backside. Then he was sticking his cock back into her pussy and pounding it again. Roni moaned as he hit her G-spot. Jack's balls slapped against her clit as his rhythm became rougher.

Roni could feel how iron-hard Jack's dick was and marveled that he could keep from coming as long as he did.

She sensed that he was nearing the breaking point and made him stop. It was time to give him what he wanted. She flipped over and had him enter her again laying on top of her.

"Hard!" she whispered urgently. "Fuck it as hard as you can."

Jack lurched into action, ramming his dick all the way inside her over and over. When he was on the edge of his orgasm, he felt Roni's fangs sink deep into his shoulder and a blinding climax, unlike anything he'd ever known soared through every cell in his body. He knew nothing but an overwhelming pleasure as his cum pumped inside her. He yelled and growled and moaned as the blissful experience seemed to last forever. Jack didn't care when he felt his own blood trickled down his chest, didn't care that Roni was drinking her fill of it. All he cared about was what she was making him feel.

Finally, the relentless feeling began to leave him and he felt a burning pain in his shoulder. He was also incredibly tired and collapsed on top of Roni.

She laughed underneath him, the sound reverberating off his chest. "Was it everything you thought it would be?"

Jack nodded and croaked, "And so much more." "You're mine, now, you know that, right?" she asked. "Yes. I understand."

"Good. Rest now," she said lightly pushing him away. "Sleep."

Jack didn't seem to have much choice. Slumber was reaching for him and he was helpless to resist it. He slept then, a smile of contentment curving his mouth.

CHAPTER 4

DARK PASSION

HE COULD SMELL the evening envelop him like the cold dark fingers he gripped his cane with. The air smelled of flesh, ripe with the smell of blood beneath. He turned to his mate, took her hand, raised it to his pointed smile, and tenderly kissed the back of her hand. It was somehow erotic to have those daggers he had drunk so deeply from in his mouth that close to the tender skin of Luciana's hand...but she too know his thirst and had shared centuries with him wishing but for one thing, to share the baby they could never have. Or could they?

They eased through the night together like two whispers fading into the shadows. Her hair as deep red as the blood they drank together in the dim moonlight. Her breasts were full and tipped with deep pink nipples, always awake, always ready to be touched. Her eyes were the startling centers of the passion she kept silent and secret within her lifeless body. Her strength was immeasurable when she would break their necks like match sticks. She was not a creature of the night, but the night lived inside her as the creature. Her speed was a flicker through the darkness, her taste upon their neck swiftly painful and then blindingly dreamlike. She was his, not because of some claim laid between them, but for the passion they shared for the ecstasy afterward as they licked each other clean from their feasting seduction. The smile on her lips was death behind a mask, and no one knew that better than Danubre...

His body was aged in truth but seductive and full of vitality and it was caught between his dark features and his refined ways. He was as tall as a horse and twice as fast. His eyes were black with the fate that lied deep in his heart. His fingers were worn from the thousands of necks he had held to his gaping jaws. When he drank of them, there was the picture of her eyes in his.

When he fed alone it was as if he came close to knowing death. There was loneliness that she filled within his soul, that is if he had had one. But he was sentenced to the dark and the vile displeasure he was forced into to survive. When they lay beside each other in their coffin, it was the sound of the sun rising in the distance that warmed their heated passion. Together they would feel their flesh cold and yet white-hot with need. The darkness was their constant companion. And when they made love in the pitch black of their bed, there would only be the animalistic growling they shared for their ecstasy.

The depth of their pleasure was that of pure devotion and the taste of mouths that only knew one dark lustful den for these two bloodsuckers. He thought of her neck not for kisses, but to grab eagerly with his heated breath to ravage her into silent surrender. There was a need upon her neck that beckoned him, a place where his lips found their home not for the blood that coursed through the veins beneath, but for the passion it awoke within his vampire princesses' skin. The taste was a yearning to feel the power surge through his body and fill his straining cock with the strength of ten men. She was his one and only eager princess and he found only her devotion...the loyalty of passion upon the wind of midnight, and the endless waning of the ebony his one true reason for living. The lust that was fostered on the lips of each other in the cold darkness of the night and the animal passion was magnetic and earth shattering. Their love was consecrated for hundreds of years the depths of the soul shared as each depends upon the very touch of the one beside them. She merely had to glance his way, for when he saw the embers of her seduction simmering in her eyes...it awakened every one of his senses.

Even though they were dark creatures of the night, the passion between them was

alluring in a macabre and beautiful kind of way. The seduction and chemistry they shared was truly magical. When he took her in his ancient arms, her cold flesh seemed to warm if even just a small amount. Love-making between these two vampires was nothing like any human had ever experienced. They had a supernatural experience each time he thrust his swollen vampire cock deep between her ivory thighs. Danubre adored Luciano and even though he had sultry and erotic charms like most vampires, he only ached and hungered for Luciano. Her pale white enchantment had captured his attention from the very beginning hundreds of years before

He remembered the first time he laid eyes upon her fair-skinned beauty. He found her alone and crying over 100 years before this very night that he was fucking her once again, but still never tired of the way her sweet and exotic pussy drew his frigidly hot cock inside of her. He truly believes that he saved the young heartbroken human he found that cold and foggy night so very long ago. He could easily fuck her 200 more years and still be completely satisfied and never have a need for another woman, either human or vampire. He only desires her enchanting beauty and extreme erotic sexuality. The union between these two lovers was unlike anything earthly. When they wound their flesh and arms around one another and came in orgasmic ecstasy together, they both screamed a sexual yet animalistic scream that could be heard for miles.

Since they were supernatural beings, they had the ability to have an orgasm and then release their vengeance at the speed of light flying through the air to their next lustful feed. As Danubre held Luciano close flying through the midnight air, he kissed the blood from her lips, felt her icy yet lovely skin against his aged hands, and fell deeper in love each and every time. As he ran his hands across her beautiful blood red nipples, he became excited and his cock became cold and hard as steel all over again. It had been this way for hundreds of years and he knew deep within his darkened heart it would be for eternity. The combination of rare but beautiful love with raw animalistic lust was the fuel that burned deep within their seething blood-starved bodies. The same passion coursed through their fangs and their flesh for one another. They had always been starved for the taste of one another and nothing human or beastly could kill that dark and illuminating passion nor could anything drive a stake through the hearts that they shared as one.

CHAPTER 5

THE INCUBUS

JESSICA HAD WAITED LONG ENOUGH. After reading sixty different magic books over five years, collecting a wide variety of tools for sorcery, and committing different mantras to memory, she felt that she was ready to do the perfect spell. She had studied a particular ritual well enough to feel comfortable with the motions and she had to see if she could be successful. She was ready to count herself among the other mages that had done the Pleasure Operation, a very ancient magic spell that had to be done correctly or the user would suffer from very dire consequences.

Jessica had set everything up in the privacy of her cold and secluded basement. She had pushed all of the extra furniture and tables out of the way. With chalk, she had drawn the symbols and protective sigils that would ensure her safety and an easy travel for the demon she would conjure. In this instance, there was only one being that she wanted to come into her circle. The demon would be an incubus-well... any incubus would do. Jessica could care less about any particular one coming, as long as they brought the right utensil.

Candles had been lit and incense was burning. The environment was appropriate for invocation. To ensure her safety, Jessica drew a circle around her. Standing in its center, she started to read from her magic book. Her thick yet healthy and agile body was naked. Her nipples were perky in the cold of the basement. She knew the spell by heart, but she didn't want to mess up, skip a beat or butcher a syllable. This had to come out perfectly, and she was guaranteed to read the spell in its proper form.

As she uttered every word, she could feel her hair standing on end and her eyes bulged with delight as she grinned. After many brushes with the supernatural world, she was going to make contact with an ethereal being in a way like she never had before.

Suddenly, even before she had finished the spell, a strong gust of wind flooded through the room. Jessica tried to stand her ground, clutching her book and stopping in mid-sentence as her hair flowed. Her nipples were so hard in the cold air, and she could hardly see as wind and dust flooded the air. It was quite temporary, however, as the wind stopped and the room seemed to be getting warmer, even a bit hot. As the woman opened her eyes, she looked before her and was surprised to see the spell had worked. Within the circle with her, a demon had gained entry. From the instant wetness she felt from the mere presence of the being, Jessica knew that the being was an incubus.

She found the being utterly attractive. With his squat body and scarily heavy muscles, the demon looked at her with a rocky head, his eyes yellow and shiny with catlike slits. Licking his lips, the demon studied Jessica from her head to her toes. He was quite happy to see that she was naked.

Jessica could see his happiness embodied in his pulsing, tall, thick erection. Jessica could hardly hide her human blushing, even as the demon looked her in the eyes and asked her the question it already knew the answer to.

"What is your desire?"

Jessica looked the demon in the eyes with a seductive look, her hand reaching down to her pussy and fingering it. "I wish to be fucked. Tell me your name."

"Silly mortal woman," the demon said as it moved in towards Jessica and held her in its arms.

"A smart demon never reveals its name." The demon started to kiss the woman on her neck and against the top of her chest.

"Oh," Jessica said as she felt the demon starting to press its face in her bosom. "I always thought a demon had to reveal its name once it was called forth."

. . .

"For that, you would need another spell. And you're much too hot and bothered for that now." The demon started licking the woman's tits. He could feel her arousal as he suckled her nipples and reached his hands against her ass.

Jessica tilted her head back. Her knees buckled and they lay on the ground, in the middle of the circle. Jessica spread her legs and allowed the demon to shove its naked cock into her

Jessica was actually surprised with how quickly the demon had started to fuck her. It was so fast and forward. Jessica wished that she could tell the demon to slow down, though it felt good, but it was so heavy to feel that cock inside of her. It was already pressing her pussy walls far apart, the demon's hands pressed against her arms. The demon's ass muscles pressed hard against each other as he fucked the woman, feeling her sweat and smelling her beautiful scent. Her pussy was already staining the ground. He really wanted her. Now, he could feel her giving him more of what he needed. Her human essence radiated in her pretty body. The demon fucked her harder and harder, her hands spanking her at some points.

"You naughty human," he said with gritted teeth as the woman moaned and screamed.

. . .

Jessica was really getting into it. With grunts, moans, and screams, she held onto the demon's sides, helping him fuck her pussy. She was getting stretched out, the length of the cock dominating her insides. She could hardly look into the demon's eyes as it dug her out. With each motion, he was hitting her g-spot without relenting. Jessica had never had such a big cock inside of her. No human cock could compare. And she was already being driven to orgasm....

She did. The woman spewed juices all over the magic circle. It was exhilarating and humiliating at the same time. Jessica had always heard stories of where humans dominated demons in their magical workings, but in her own situation, she felt like it was the other way around. This incubus was dominating her, and she liked it.

Jessica must have had an orgasm two or three times before they both came to an absolute stop.

Jessica lay wet and sweaty, trying to catch her breath as the demon laid on top of her.

The demon rubbed the woman's chin. "Now, the operation is complete." Jessica looked into the demon's eyes. "What happens now?"

The demon grinned as he moved his hands through the woman's hair. "Well... since you were not strong enough to finish the entire spell from start to finish, you will be mine You will work as my sexual slave and will grant me access to your pussy whenever I desire it or call for it."

. . .

Jessica nodded. There was a sense of embarrassment in being owned but a sense of excitement too. "I can do that."

"Good." The demon said as he pressed his finger against one of Jessica's nipples and played with it. "Now, we break, and in a few minutes, we'll play some more."

ABOUT THE AUTHOR

Blaine Teller is an emerging erotica author of many erotica kinks and sub-genres. Be sure to check out other books and leave a review if this story got you hot!

Visit my blog at Blaine Teller's Blog

Join my newsletter for the exclusive Blaine Teller's Newsletter

Sign up for Free Stories from Xplicit Press Authors

Xplicit Press Author Updates

Like Xplicit Press on Facebook

Follow Xplicit Press on Twitter

Readers: I want to expand a few of the stories to see where the characters can be explored further. If there are any of the stories that you would like to read more about again, I'd love to hear from you!

Keep In Touch
Blaine Teller
info@blaineteller.com

www.ingramcontent.com/pod-product-compliance
Lightning Source LLC
Chambersburg PA
CBHW020814130626
46554CB00006B/2425